THE ROOSTER
WHO UNDERSTOOD
JAPANESE

For Barbara and Steve
Kathy, Kenny, and Margo

THE ROOSTER
WHO UNDERSTOOD
JAPANESE

by Yoshiko Uchida

Illustrated by Charles Robinson

Charles Scribner's Sons   New York

Text copyright © 1976 Yoshiko Uchida
Illustrations copyright © 1976
Charles Robinson

Copyright under the Berne Convention

All rights reserved.

1 3 5 7 9 11 13 15 17 19 RD/C
20 18 16 14 12 10 8 6 4 2

Printed in the United States of America
Library of Congress Catalog Card
Number 76-13450
ISBN 0-684-14672-X

"Mrs. K.!" Miyo called. "I'm here!"

Every afternoon when Miyo came home from school, where she was in the third grade, she went to the home of her neighbor, Mrs. Kitamura, whom she called "Mrs. K."

This was because Miyo's mother was a doctor at University Hospital and didn't get home until supper time. Sometimes, she didn't get home even then, and if she didn't, Miyo just stayed on at Mrs. K's.

It was a fine arrangement all around because Mrs. Kitamura was a widow, and she enjoyed Miyo's company. Not that she was lonely. She had a basset hound named Jefferson, a ten-year-old parrot named Hamilton, a coal black cat named Leonardo, and a pet rooster named Mr. Lincoln. She talked to all of them in Japanese. She also talked to the onions and potatoes she'd planted in her front yard instead of a lawn, coaxing them each day to grow plump and delicious.

About the time Miyo came home from school, Mrs. K. was usually outside talking to her potatoes and onions, but today Mrs. K. was nowhere to be seen. She wasn't out front, and she wasn't in back talking to any of her animals either.

Her dog, Jefferson, stretched sleepily and came to greet Miyo as she opened the gate to the backyard.

"Hello, Jefferson Kitamura," Miyo said. "Where's Mrs. K.?"

Jefferson wagged his tail and sniffed at Miyo. Then he went back to his special spot at the foot of the willow tree and curled up to get on with his afternoon nap.

Miyo stopped next to see Mr. Lincoln. He was strutting about in his pen making rooster-like sounds and looking very intelligent and dignified. Mrs. K. had told Miyo that he understood every word she said to him whether she spoke in English or Japanese.

"Mrs. Kitamura, *doko*?" Miyo said, asking Mr. Lincoln where she was.

He cocked his head, looked at her with his small bright eyes, and uttered a squawking sound.

Miyo shrugged. Maybe Mr. Lincoln did understand Japanese, but it certainly didn't do her any good if she couldn't understand what he said back to her.

"Never mind," she said. "I'll find her." And she hurried toward the brown shingled house covered with ivy that hung over it like droopy hair. The back door was unlatched, and Miyo walked in.

"Mrs. K., I'm here," she called once more.

Immediately a high shrill voice repeated, "Mrs. K., I'm here." It was Hamilton, the parrot, who lived in a big gold cage in Mrs. Kitamura's kitchen.

"Hello, Hamilton," Miyo said.

"Hello, Hamilton," he answered back.

Miyo sniffed as she walked through the kitchen, hoping she might smell chocolate brownies or freshly baked bread. But today there were no nice welcoming smells at all. There was only silence and the smell of floor wax.

Miyo went through the swinging doors into the dining room and found Mrs. K. sitting at the big oval dining room table. She still wore her floppy gardening hat over the pile of gray hair that had been frizzled by a home permanent, and she was doing something Miyo had never seen her do before. She was making herself a cup of ceremonial Japanese tea, whipping up the special powdered green tea in a beautiful tea bowl with a small bamboo whisk.

Miyo knew exactly what Mrs. K. was doing because she had seen a lady in a silk kimono perform the Japanese tea ceremony at the Buddhist temple just last month.

Somehow Mrs. K. didn't look quite right preparing the tea in her gardening smock and floppy hat, sitting at a table piled high with old newspapers and magazines. Furthermore, she was frowning, and Miyo knew the tea ceremony was supposed to make one feel peaceful and calm.

"*Mah!*" Mrs. K. said, looking startled. "I was so busy with my thoughts, I didn't even hear you come in."

Miyo looked at the pale green froth of tea in the tea bowl, knowing it was strong and bitter. "Is that our afternoon tea?" she asked, trying not to look too disappointed.

"No, no, not yours," Mrs. K. answered quickly. "Just mine. I made it to calm myself." She turned the bowl around carefully and drank it in the proper three and a half sips. "There," she sighed.

"Are you calm now?"

Mrs. K. shook her head. "Not really. Actually, not at all. As a matter of fact, I am most upset."

Mrs. Kitamura stood up and started toward the kitchen, and Leonardo appeared from beneath her chair to follow close behind. Miyo thought that was a strange name for a cat, but Mrs. K. had told her he was a very sensitive, creative cat, and she had named him after Leonardo da Vinci.

In fact, all of Mrs. K's pets had very elegant and dignified names which she had chosen after going to a class in American history in order to become an American citizen. She said animals were purer in spirit than most human beings and deserved names that befit their character. "Besides," she had added, "I like to be different."

Mrs. K. certainly was different, all right. She wasn't at all like most of the other elderly ladies who went to the Japanese Buddhist temple.

"It is because I am a free spirit," she had explained to Miyo one day.

Maybe it was because she had lived in America so much longer than the other ladies who had come from Japan. She never did anything she didn't want to do, although she was always careful not to cause anyone any grief.

Miyo wondered now why Mrs. K. was so upset. Usually she was full of fun, but today she scarcely smiled at Miyo.

"I've been upset since seven o'clock this morning," she explained suddenly.

"Why?" Miyo asked, gratefully accepting a glass of milk and some peanut butter cookies. "Did you get out of the wrong side of bed?"

That was what her mother sometimes asked when Miyo was grumpy. But that wasn't Mrs. K's trouble at all.

"It's not me," she said. "It's my new neighbor, Mr. Wickett. He told me that if Mr. Lincoln didn't stop waking him up by crowing at six in the morning, he was going to report me to the police for disturbing the peace! Can you imagine anything so un-friendly?"

Miyo certainly couldn't. "He's mean," she said.

"What am I going to do?" Mrs. K. asked, as though Miyo were the wise old woman in the Japanese tale who could answer any puzzling question put to her.

"I can't go out and tell Mr. Lincoln he is not to crow anymore. That would be like telling Jefferson not to wag his tail, or telling Leonardo not to groom himself . . ."

"Or telling Hamilton not to mimic us," Miyo said, getting into the spirit of things.

"Exactly," Mrs. K. agreed. "He is only behaving in his natural rooster-like way. And besides," she added, "any respectable old man should be up by six o'clock. You and your mama have never complained."

Miyo didn't say that they were already up at six o'clock anyway. She wondered what she could say to make Mrs. K. feel better, and finally she said, "I'll ask my mother. She'll know what to do."

Miyo's mother usually found a way to solve most problems. She had to because Miyo had no father, and there was no one else in their house to ask. Miyo's father had died long ago and Miyo barely remembered him.

"Don't worry, Mama will think of something," Miyo said as she left Mrs. Kitamura's house.

Mrs. K. nodded. "I hope so," she said dismally. "In the meantime, I must think of something before six o'clock tomorrow morning."

When Miyo got home, Mother was just starting supper. "Hi sweetie," she called. "How was Mrs. K.?"

"She was worried," Miyo answered as she began to set the table. "She's got to make Mr. Lincoln stop crowing."

"Whatever for?"

Miyo quickly told Mother about Mr. Wickett. "He's a mean old man," she said, scowling at the thought of him. "Mr. Lincoln doesn't hurt anybody."

But Mother said, "Well, I can see Mr. Wickett's side too. If I could sleep late, I'm not so sure I'd like having a rooster wake me at six o'clock. Besides," she added, "our town is growing, and we're in the city limits now. Maybe Mrs. K. will just have to give Mr. Lincoln away."

Miyo didn't even want to think of such a thing. "But he's not just any old rooster," she objected.

He certainly wasn't. Mrs. K. had raised him since he was a baby chick, thinking that he was going to become a hen and give her an egg for breakfast every day.

"Besides," she added, "he doesn't crow very loud."

Mother nodded sympathetically. "I know," she said. "Well, maybe we can think of something."

But nobody could. Not mother, not Miyo, nor Mrs. K.

Miyo felt that neither she nor her mother really deserved the *osushi*, for they hadn't come up with a single good idea to help Mrs. K. But neither had Mr. Kitamura, and he got a small dish of *osushi* too. Mrs. K. had put it in front of his photograph that stood beside the black and gold altar with the small statue of Buddha and the incense and candle.

In fact, ever since he died years ago, Mr. Kitamura always got a small dish of anything good that Mrs. K. made, and Miyo wondered if he came down from the Pure Land in the middle of the night to eat it. Mrs. K. told her, however, that the food was for his spirit, and that it reached him just as her love and thoughts did, in a wonderful way that she couldn't quite explain.

"I do wish we could think of a way to help Mrs. K.," Mother said as they ate Mrs. K's delicious *osushi* and drank steaming cups of tea.

But Mother was so tired at the end of a long day looking after sick babies and children at the hospital that she just couldn't find any good ideas inside her head. She did say, however, that keeping Mr. Lincoln inside a carton in the house was not the answer.

And Mrs. K. certainly found out it wasn't. On the second night she brought him inside, Mr. Lincoln poked his way right out of the carton and walked all over her house. He scratched the floors and pecked at her sofa and got into a fight with Leonardo, the cat. By the time Mrs. K. got to them, there were feathers all over her living room and Leonardo almost had fresh chicken for breakfast.

"I suppose I will have to give Mr. Lincoln away," Mrs. K. murmured sadly. "But I can't give him to just anybody. It has to be someone who will love him and not turn him into fricassee or stew."

Mrs. K. lost three pounds from worrying and said she was becoming a nervous wreck. "If I can't find a new home for Mr. Lincoln, I suppose I will simply have to go to jail," she said, trying to look brave.

Miyo thought and thought until her jaws ached. How in the world could they find just the right person to take Mr. Lincoln? Then, suddenly, she had an idea.

"I know," she said brightly. "I'll put an ad in our class mag-azine."

Mrs. K. thought about it. "Well," she said slowly, "I suppose it won't do any harm."

What she really meant was that it probably wouldn't do any good either. But Miyo was determined to try. She had to hurry for Mrs. K. had already said several times that she was becoming a nervous wreck, and Miyo certainly didn't want her to stop being the nice, cheerful person she was.

Miyo's class magazine was almost ready to be mimeographed for the month of October. There were several sections, one each for news, feature stories, science, sports, book reviews, poetry, and, finally, a small section for ads. That's where Miyo thought Mr. Lincoln would fit nicely.

She made her ad very special. She wrote, "WANTED: NICE HOME FOR FRIENDLY, INTELLIGENT, DIGNIFIED ROOSTER. P.S. HE UNDERSTANDS JAPANESE." Then she added, "PLEASE HURRY! URGENT!"

Her teacher, Mrs. Fielding, told her it was a fine ad, and sug-gested that she include her phone number, so Miyo did. She also drew a picture of Mr. Lincoln beneath her ad, trying to make him look dignified and friendly.

The magazine came out on September 30. That very after-noon, a policeman rang the doorbell of Mrs. K's shaggy ivy-covered house.

"I've a complaint, Ma'm," he said, "about a rooster?" He seemed to think there might have been some mistake.

Mrs. K. sighed. "Come inside, officer," she said. "I've been expecting you." She supposed now she would just have to go quietly to jail, but first she wanted a cup of tea. "Would you like some tea?" she asked.

Officer McArdle was tired and his feet hurt. "Thank you, Ma'm," he said, and he came inside. He looked all around at Mrs. Kitamura's home, bulging with Japanese things he'd never seen before. There were Japanese dolls dancing inside dusty glass cases. There were scrolls of Japanese paintings hanging on the walls. There was the black and gold Buddhist altar, and spread out all over the dining room table were Japanese books and newspapers. Mrs. K. pushed them aside and put down a tray of tea and cookies.

"*Dozo*," she said, "please have some tea." She took off her apron and smoothed down her frizzy gray hair. Then she told Officer McArdle all about her troubles with Mr. Lincoln.

He looked sympathetic, but he said, "You're breaking a city law by having a rooster in your yard. You really should be fined, you know."

Mrs. K. was astonished. "Even if I am only barely inside the city limits?"

Officer McArdle nodded. "I'm afraid so. I'll give you two more days to get rid of your rooster. Mr. Wickett says you're disturbing the peace."

Then he thanked her for the tea and cookies and he was gone.

Miyo was proud of the ad in her class magazine, but no one seemed at all interested in Mr. Lincoln. Instead, several people told her how much they liked her feature story about Mr. Botts, the school custodian, who was retiring.

She had written, "Say good-bye to the best custodian Hawthorn School ever had. Mr. Botts is retiring because he is getting tired. At the age of sixty-five, who wouldn't? He and Mrs. Botts are going to Far Creek. He is going to eat a lot and sleep a lot and maybe go fishing. So, so long, Mr. Botts. And good luck!"

Her teacher, Mrs. Fielding, told her it was a fine story.

On her way home, Miyo ran into Mr. Botts himself. He told her it was the first time in his entire life that anyone had written a feature story about him.

When he got home that night, he took off his shoes, sat in his favorite chair, lit a pipe, and read the magazine from cover to cover. At the bottom of page twenty, he saw Miyo's ad about Mr. Lincoln.

"Tami," he said to Mrs. Botts, who happened to be Japanese, "how would you like to have a rooster?"

"A what?"

"A rooster," Mr. Botts repeated. "One that understands Japanese."

Mrs. Botts thought that Mr. Botts had had too much excitement, what with his retirement party at school and all. But he kept right on talking.

"When we move to Far Creek, didn't you say you were going to grow vegetables and raise chickens while I go hunting and fishing?"

Mrs. Botts remembered having said something like that. "Yes, I guess I did."

"Well, if you're going to raise chickens, you'll need a rooster."

"Why, I guess that's so."

"Then we might as well have one that's friendly and dignified," Mr. Botts said, and he went right to the telephone to call Miyo.

"I'll take that rooster you want to find a home for," he said. "My wife, Tami, could talk to it in Japanese too."

Miyo couldn't believe it. Someone had actually read her ad and that someone was Mr. Botts and his wife. They would give Mr. Lincoln a fine home and surely wouldn't turn him into fricassee or stew. At last, she had done something to help Mrs. K. and keep her from becoming a nervous wreck. As soon as she told Mother, she ran right over to tell Mrs. K. the good news.

Mrs. K. was just about to stuff Mr. Lincoln into a wooden crate for the night. When Miyo told her that Mr. Lincoln would have a nice half-Japanese home in Far Creek with Mr. and Mrs. Botts, Mrs. K. gave Miyo such a hug she almost squeezed the breath out of her.

"Hooray! *Banzai!*" Mrs. K. said happily. "Tomorrow we will have a party to celebrate. I shall invite you and your mama, and Mr. and Mrs. Botts." And because Mrs. K. felt so relieved and happy, she even decided to invite Mr. Wickett.

"Even though you are a cross old man," she said to him, "I suppose you were right. A rooster shouldn't live in a small pen at the edge of town. He should live in the country where he'll have some hens to talk to and nobody will care if he crows at the sun."

Mr. Wickett was a little embarrassed to come to Mrs. K's party, but he was too lonely to say no. He came with a box of chocolate-dipped cherries and said, "I'm sorry I caused such a commotion."

But Mrs. K. told him he needn't be sorry. "Life needs a little stirring up now and then," she admitted. "Besides," she added, "now both Mr. Lincoln and I have found new friends."

Miyo and her mother brought a caramel cake with Mr. Lincoln's initials on it and Mr. and Mrs. Botts brought Mrs. K. a philodendron plant. "Maybe you can talk to it in Japanese now instead of to Mr. Lincoln," Mrs. Botts said, "and don't worry, I'll take good care of him."

"You come on out to visit us and your rooster any time you like," Mr. Botts added.

Miyo's mother promised that one day soon she would drive them all up to Far Creek to see how Mr. Lincoln liked his new home.

When the party was over, Mr. Botts carried Mr. Lincoln in his crate to his station wagon. Mr. Lincoln gave a polite squawk of farewell and Mrs. K. promised she would come visit him soon.

"Good-bye, Mr. Lincoln. Good-bye, Mr. and Mrs. Botts," Miyo called.

From inside Mrs. K's kitchen, Hamilton, the parrot, screeched. "Good-bye, Mr. Lincoln. Good-bye."

Jefferson roused himself from his bed near the stove and came outside to wag his tail at everybody, and Leonardo rubbed up against Mrs. K's legs to remind her that he was still there.

Then Mr. Botts honked his horn and they were gone.

"I hope we'll see each other again soon," Mr. Wickett said to Mrs. K.

"Good night, Mr. Wickett," she answered. "I'm sure we will."

Miyo and her mother thanked Mrs. K. for the nice party and went home, leaving her to say good night to her potatoes and onions before going inside.

"Do you think she'll miss Mr. Lincoln a lot?" Miyo asked.

"She will for a while," Mother answered, "but now she has a new friend and neighbor to talk to."

Miyo nodded. That was true. And even if Mr. Wickett couldn't understand Japanese, at least he could answer back, and maybe that was even better than having an intelligent rooster around.

Miyo was glad everything had turned out so well, and went to bed feeling good inside.

"Good night, Mama," she called softly to her mother.

"Good night, Miyo," Mother answered as she tucked her in.

Then, one by one, the lights went out in all the houses along the street, and soon only the sounds of the insects filled the dark night air.